WARNING

This book contains adult language and violence. It may be considered offensive to some readers. This book is for sale to adults ONLY.

* * * * * * * * * * * * * * * * * *

Please store your files wisely where they cannot be accessed by underage readers.

ISBN-13: 978-1773500751
ISBN-10: 1773500759

Other Books by Freddie Kim:

The Time Guardian Thriller Series

When the Time Guardian goes missing, it is up to Sonia to travel back to the past the rectify the future of humanity. Follow this epic tale of good versus evil in the battle to control Earth's destiny.

Stinger Jacked

The Free Humanity Movement (FHM) resistance hatches a plan to steal a Stinger Class assault ship from OmniClon Universal (OCU) and its alliance partner, the ka'Thar. With morale at an all-time low, Rogal and his team of misfits are sent on what could potentially be a suicide mission.

Get the latest update on new releases from the author at:

https://www.freddiekim.com/newsletter/

This book is Part One of the "The Cyber Heist Files"

Book 1 – Cyber Heist

The entire financial industry of the World Government is at risk when a weaponized virus is covertly uploaded into the computer system. Faced with an imminent crisis, the government releases the whistle blower, Tyler Wilkens, in exchange for eradicating the virus that has infected their computer systems. Something malevolent is afoot and Wilkens is the best chance the government has to combat it.

Book 2 – Kill Code

When Tyler Wilkens fails to completely eradicate the virus, he is put back in prison and his competitor, another tech company, is tasked with finishing the job. As circumstances turn dire, Wilkens is released once again to do the government's bidding. But what he finds within the computer system is something ominous and unexpected. Will Wilkens be able to save the World Government from complete financial collapse?

Book 3 – Coup D'état

With the World Government ousted in the coup d'état, OmniClon Universal (OCU) attempts to take control over the world. Tasked with finding evidence to save the former government, Wilkens falls deep down the rabbit hole. With the help of Monica Franchette, Wilkens uncovers a conspiracy that leads him to multiple assassinations and the highest levels of authority. The burden of truth does not come without its risks. Will Wilkens be a marked man with a target on his back for the rest of his life?

The Cyber Heist Files

Cyber Heist

Book One

By Freddie Kim

Table of Contents

Chapter One

GIORGIO KEPT his eye on the red LED numbers of the clock on the wall. It read 4:58 PM and seemed to have been stuck at that time for the past two minutes while he closed all the applications on his holo-screen. The droning sounds on the office floor had already died down as others closed their workstations and prepared to leave. He was getting impatient. Why are the last two minutes before the start of a long weekend always the longest?

The administrative offices of the World Government were going to be closed for three days. Giorgio had his entire weekend planned, but it depended on him making it on the next shuttle out. If he missed this one, then the fifteen-minute wait for the next shuttle would mean he would miss his 5:45 PM flight to Parisio. Because of the long weekend, the next available flight wouldn't arrive at the vacation city until well after midnight.

Sharla was already in Parisio, waiting in the luxury suite Giorgio had booked months before. He had planned a romantic evening, starting with dinner and then dancing. *Dessert* would surely follow later, something he was looking forward to more than an expensive dinner.

When the clock changed to 4:59 PM, he breathed a sigh of relief and pulled out his briefcase, ready to dash out of the office in less than a minute. His co-workers were already starting to move toward the exit doors. That was when his computer uttered a small 'bleep' and his holo-screen lit up from sleep mode.

Giorgio stared at the flashing icon on the computer screen. "Dammit. Wonder what that's all about?" he said mainly to himself. There was a glitch in the waste management system. These server farms, can't live with them, can't trash them. When they were first implemented way back when, they worked beautifully. Very few problems and only a small number of hiccups here and there.

Over the years, as capacity was added to handle new divisions, increased traffic, and data processing, the piecemeal build in the system architecture resulted in the use of patches to mend the seams between various systems. But the damn patches weren't meant as a long-term solution. Each one weakened the whole system.

As per protocol, Giorgio called his supervisor, Clarence, who was not going to be happy after last month's cyber fiasco. He hoped Clarence was still in his office. Otherwise, he would have to call his supervisor on the emergency line.

From past experience, Giorgio knew Clarence would never answer his emergency personal communicator outside of work and preferred to respond to voicemail at his leisure. It could mean at least a half-hour delay before Clarence would return the call. Hating himself for not ignoring the glitch and dashing out the door, Giorgio held his breath as he listened for the line to connect on the other side. One, two, three rings.

Giorgio heard the line pick up on the other side and he let out a silent breath of relief.

"What is it?" asked Clarence.

"I have a flashing icon on my screen in the waste management system," said Giorgio in a terse voice.

"What do you think it is?"

"I don't know. I haven't seen this one before. It could be the same damn crap. Should we do like before?" asked Giorgio.

"Check the Diagnostics folder. There's a new program you can initiate. It should take care of the glitch," said Clarence.

Clarence had been the system's supervisor for years, and he'd seen these types of things before. It was a pain to have to deal with these annoyances over and over again. They were always minor glitches in the system, easily taken care of by running a diagnostic program and then a simple patch program. Just one patch over another over another. It was like painting layers on a wall, it just made it easier to pick off chips.

The new program was a combination diagnostic and self-repairing program that created simple patches to fix minor glitches. It was quick and dirty, requiring little intervention from expensive programmers. The incident would automatically be logged, and somebody would collect all the occurrences of glitches and problems with the system for the master programmers to consider when building the next upgrade.

"Okay, running diagnostics now," said Giorgio, trying to keep the anger out of his tone. He had missed his shuttle, so he decided to hunker down and wait patiently for the program to run its course.

The holo-screen came back to life, and the computer speaker sounded out a soft 'bleep.'

Giorgio looked over from his workstation monitor. An hour had passed, and the self-repairing diagnostic program signaled the completion of its task. The waste management system seemed to be working alright, the glitch was gone. Giorgio closed the file on the glitch and noted it in his incident report, a report that probably no one·would read. Hopefully, the glitch would not occur again, but no one was holding their breath.

He looked at the wall clock. It read 6:49 PM. He had time to catch the shuttle to the aerial port. He wouldn't be getting in to Parisio until after midnight, but Sharla would be waiting up for him. He would still have time for dessert, after all, assuming she was still in the mood and not angry. And if she wasn't in the mood, he had the whole weekend to make it up to her. Fortunately for him, the romantic ambience of the scenic city would be doing the heavy lifting for him.

As he packed up his things to leave, the phone rang. Dammit, who would call this late at the start of a long weekend? Again, Giorgio felt tempted to leave, but his conscience got the better of him.

The call was coming in from the Procurement Division. Giorgio picked up the phone.

"Hey, Henry. What's up?"

"Oh good. You're still there," said Henry.

"Long story and I was just about to go. Make it fast," said Giorgio, frustration showing through in his voice. There was no way he was going to miss the next shuttle.

"Oh sorry. I'm seeing an anomaly in our system," said Henry in his usual slow drawl. "Can you take a look to see if you can fix it before we start to worry?"

Giorgio pulled up the holo-screen and swiped it over to show the Procurement system configuration. Sure enough, there was another freaking glitch in the system. One of the icons was flashing. Giorgio considered calling his supervisor again, but this was a clear case of the same situation he had just experienced.

"Henry, I've seen this before. Run a diagnostic on that system. I'll send you the file. It should be an easy fix. Nothing major to worry about."

"Thanks, Giorgio. I knew I could count on you," Henry said. "Have a good weekend."

He hung up the phone and sent the file to Henry's workstation through the government intranet. Giorgio was relieved the issue could be fixed with a simple program. After all, he had a weekend date with his girlfriend and tonight was going to be a special night for him. The thought of seeing her in the next few hours lifted his spirits and put a smile on his face. Wouldn't want to ruin it with a stupid computer system problem. Once the patch was applied, the system seemed to be back to normal.

Before Giorgio left the office once and for all, he had what he thought was a stroke of genius. He quickly composed a memo and sent it out to all division heads and supervisors with the new self-repairing diagnostic program attached. That way, if the glitch showed up again over the weekend, the various divisions could do their own repairs without having to bother him.

As he hit <Send> on his workstation, he felt a great weight lift from his shoulders. He was sure he had saved the government computer systems from a potential threat.

Giorgio was finally on his way to a well-deserved long weekend.

Chapter Two

Monica looked up from her workstation as it emitted a soft 'bleep' and her holo-screen lit up. She chuckled to herself as she read the memo from Central Systems. It was from Giorgio Karpati.

"Hey, did you see this crap?" she yelled over to the adjoining room. Through the clear acrylic window separating the two rooms, she could see the back of Craig's head and his holo-screen showing the same memo.

Craig turned his head and gave Monica a big grin. "Yep, they have no idea." Like Monica, he felt revulsion for Giorgio and his judgmental crew.

Though it was the start of Craig's weekend shift and Monica wasn't required to be there, she was content to stay. She preferred the company of machines to the people outside of work, so she spent most of her waking hours in the office. It was her prerogative. She was the boss.

With her right middle finger extended, she hit the keyboard and whispered, "Delete, delete." The memo disappeared forever from the holo-screen.

Monica Franchette, or the MF Overlord as her small team affectionately called her, looked over at the bank of L-KAT mainframe computers in the cool server room. She had been head of the division since they were first purchased. These were her babies, these massive machines. Her pride and joy.

Monica was the last of her breed, a government-employed mainframe technician. The only full-timer of her kind that the World Government had kept. That was because her division was a mistake. The original plan was to develop a mainframe backbone to govern all of the World Government's processing services and databases. But that plan had changed.

It changed when the head of the Procurement Division, Saul Pendleton, negotiated a better deal with Virtual Sentinel Technologies (VST) and awarded them the contract to supply and build an extensive network of server farms for all of the government's divisions and services.

So now the four mainframes were relegated to serve as databases for the world's registry of citizens which included information such as purchase habits of every inhabitant on Earth, DNA makeup, family tree, and other individual traits. All this information was collected through the many points of input throughout the world such as medical records, bank transactions, item purchases, teacher evaluations, classroom records, and travel history.

The L-KATs communicated with the server farms, providing real-time information when called upon.

Monica walked into the server room and ran her hand over the smooth black metal cover of one of the machines, like a loving mother caressing the tender cheek of her toddler. These old L-KAT mainframes were 34th generation ZxZ series, but they ran as smooth as the first day they were activated. Monica felt the coolness of the metal cover, the vibration of activity beneath barely perceptible to her touch.

Purring like a kitten, she said, "How are my Hell-Kats today? You don't need no stinking self-repairing diagnostic program when you have me, do you?"

Yes, she even named each one. Hell-Kat One, Two, Three, and Four.

Without even looking, Craig knew she was caressing her machines. He had witnessed it before and felt embarrassed for her. Fortunately, their division received very few visitors. When he heard her murmuring to them, he shook his head slowly from side to side and continued surfing the internet.

Chapter Three

It wasn't until the end of the following week that Clarence took the time to look at the status reports. It took him a while, but he saw a disturbing trend. "That can't be right," he said as he thumbed through the reports again to confirm his suspicions. He picked up the phone and rang Giorgio.

"Can you explain these status reports?" asked Clarence.

"After that initial glitch, boss, I started getting reports from other divisions. I sent out that self-repairing diagnostic program you gave me to everyone. Looks like it fixed the glitch so no worries," said Giorgio, who thought he had done the absolute correct thing and didn't understand what the big deal was.

"We started getting all these glitches, and you failed to let me know right away?" asked Clarence. He was annoyed with his underling, and didn't bother to hide it in his voice.

"No, I just got one call. I sent the program to everyone after that." Confused, Giorgio was hoping his supervisor would see the wisdom of his action.

"Did you know there were over two thousand occurrences? The alarm bells should have been set off after three occurrences." Clarence's voice increased in intensity and pitch, hoping the severity of the situation would sink in under the thick skull of his underling.

"Sorry, boss, I called about the first one, and when you said to use the new program, I thought it would be fine to use if the problem was the same. I'll notify you next time if it happens again," said Giorgio. Dang, it's not like he didn't follow protocol. Now his supervisor was annoyed at some small glitch that had been taken care of by a program that his office approved. Giorgio felt like he just couldn't win, and it annoyed him to no end.

Clarence hung up the phone and stared at the reports, wishing he could stop the rising fear that something wasn't quite right, and shit was going to hit the server cooling fans.

"You assured me that your company would take care of everything," said Saul.

As head of the Procurement Division, it was Saul's decision to purchase and implement the server farms. The report of the recent spate of glitches had gotten him worried. It would mean his head if they couldn't get ahead of the problem and find its source. But for now, the government systems were all performing normally.

"We're doing everything we can," said Randall. "We have our best guy on it."

Randall Easton was the Chief Client Liaison Officer for VST, and he was the one who convinced Saul that his company could deliver what the government needed. Beneath his cool, confident façade was a man close to panic mode. His heart was beating rapidly, and his hands were sweating. If he couldn't get Saul to calm down, then their little arrangement could be exposed.

"Well, your best guy isn't doing the job," said Saul. "If you guys can't solve this problem, that'll be the end of our contract with your company."

"Don't think I'm the only one who will be going down for this," said Randall aggressively. "You're the one who pressured us into lowering our prices. Plus, that extra incentive you requested won't look too good to the President, now will it?"

"Do you think you can mess with me?" said Saul vehemently.

"All I'm saying is that it'll be beneficial for us both if we work together on this, instead of against one another."

"I get it. And all I am saying is that if this happens again, I won't be able to keep Clarence from digging further into the matter." Saul threw his arms up in exasperation, feeling helpless and ineffective.

"All I can tell you is that we'll try our best. Be prepared to bail if you can. I can have a shuttle waiting for you just in case it escalates into something we're not able to stop," said Randall.

<<<>>>

As Clarence studied the status reports, he realized there was something he had missed earlier. He slapped himself on the forehead. "Damn, why didn't I see this before?"

"Tell me," said Victor, eyebrows raised in anticipation for the answer. Victor Nugent was the head programmer for VST and was assigned to the government on high-priority cases.

"Only the systems supported by the service farms were affected by the glitch. The old mainframes held their own," said Clarence, loathing coming through in his voice.

He could just see it now. The MF Overlord gloating over the superiority of her machines. He and Monica never really got along, they had always been rivals, championing the advantages of their computer systems over each other. Up to now, Clarence was the clear winner if one were to judge based on the size and budget allocation of the government resources. But the new insight would bring that into question.

"Why do you think that is?" asked Clarence with some suspicion. Clarence raised his eyebrows, anxiously waiting for an answer from the head programmer.

"It looks like a new type of virus," said Victor. "When we track the glitch pattern, we can see it was introduced through the waste management system. Someone must have uploaded the virus to one of the stations. Our safety protocols missed it somehow. Maybe it was disguised or morphed after it entered the server bank. Let me see if I can decode it right now."

Victor fed the code fragment through his debugger and shook his head in a skeptical double-take. "This can't be right."

"What can't be right?" asked Clarence.

"This code fragment. I recognize it, but I don't know how it got here."

"Please explain." Clarence gave his eager attention to what Victor was going to say.

"Have you heard of the SNFR worm?" Victor hesitated then continued. "Otherwise known as the sniffer worm in the industry?"

Clarence shook his head, perplexed. "Never heard of it."

"The code fragment is part of the engine core of that worm. The sniffer worm was developed by one of our very own programmers, under contract to the World Government. It was meant to be used under limited conditions for the purposes of forensic auditing and for exposing activities of known terrorists and enemies of the World citizens." Victor paused, grabbed his bottle of water and took a few gulps.

"Is that a bad thing?" asked Clarence.

"No, that part is fine. It's the next part that is disconcerting. Anyway, the sniffer worm was so effective in what it did that the World Government used it to covertly sniff out every detail of every citizen who had an electronic footprint, so basically everyone."

"This code fragment was used to get this virus into places where it shouldn't go?" Shivers ran down Clarence's spine as he realized the extent of the threat.

"Exactly."

"If one your programmers developed it, then it should be easy enough to get him to look at this virus and find a way to disable it," said Clarence.

"Not so simple. Remember I said the Government used the sniffer worm covertly?"

"Yes, about that. If it was done covertly, should you be telling me all this?"

"See that's the thing. Have you ever heard of the name, Tyler Wilkens?"

"Tyler Wilkens, the traitor? Who hasn't? He divulged government secrets and was convicted for it. He deserves all the time he got," said Clarence in a disapproving tone.

"It's not that simple. He exposed the covert use of his program by the government. The government was spying on their own citizens."

Clarence shuddered with revulsion at Victor's words.

Chapter Four

Tyler Wilkens tossed the squash ball against the concrete floor. He watched it bounce up against the wall and arc back to his outstretched hand as he sat, leaning against the metal rack of his cot. One hundred. He repeated the action. One hundred and one. His goal today was to reach one thousand. He had almost reached it yesterday but meal time had broken his concentration. Today he started earlier, but he was already getting bored.

The clanking of a key at the metal door lock offered a reprieve from his regular daily routine. He wondered what that could be all about.

As two guards entered his cell, he put his arms together and extended them outward. The guards placed metal clasps around his wrists and ankles.

With one guard in front of him and the other behind, he followed the lead guard to the interrogation room.

"What's the catch? What do I get out of it?" asked Tyler. After an undetermined amount of time spent in confinement, he was astonished and couldn't believe his ears.

"We're offering you a chance to spend the rest of your sentence under house arrest, away from that concrete cage you call home," said Felix Switzer. His face remained stoic.

Tyler sensed that the Assistant Attorney General was under a lot of pressure. Why else would they send him to make a deal? Tyler's heart raced at the thought of a transfer. Then reality kicked in. He would still not be free.

"Why should I trust you? You were the one who put me here in the first place." Tyler's face furrowed into a frown. Now he was getting angry.

"If you do this, you will demonstrate repentance, and the government is prepared to show leniency. We might be able to forgive your transgressions and push for a lighter sentence," Felix relaxed his facial muscles and tried to give his most sincere look.

"No, I was betrayed by my government once. Spying on your own citizens isn't something a just government does. Passing a law to make it legal after the fact should not have been allowed. If I do this, I want a full pardon. And I have a list of conditions that need to be met." This time, Tyler spoke with more force behind the words. After all. He really had nothing to lose.

The Assistant Attorney General gave a slow, heavy sigh and stood up. "Very well, have it your way." With that, he nodded at the guard who then took Tyler by the arm and escorted him back to his cold concrete cell.

Later that night as Tyler tried to get some sleep, he heard the familiar clanking of a metal key turning in the metal door lock. He thought they might be coming to beat him severely. Maybe to death.

Two guards entered. Tyler stood up, still exhausted from his earlier ordeal. He extended his arms for the wrist restraints.

"We're not here for that," said one of the guards.

The other guard tossed a large heavy paper bag at Tyler. The prisoner had a look of confusion on his face.

The first guard looked at the second guard, and they both chuckled. Then the first guard looked at Tyler and said, "Get dressed. You got your damn pardon."

Chapter Five

Clarence and Victor sat silently by the work bench as Tyler checked the monitors and computer systems in the central control room. It didn't look like he was doing much. Clarence and Victor thought he was yanking their chain until they heard a knock at the door.

"Ah, that should be my kit," said Tyler. "Would you be so kind as to retrieve it from the courier?" He looked at both men expectantly.

"I'll get it." Victor got up and answered the door. In a moment, he was back with a heavy large duffel bag. It looked worn and smelled of moth balls.

"The government confiscated all my equipment during my internment. Fortunately, it is proprietary hardware, and no one else would have a clue about how to use it."

Tyler unzipped the bag and dug around inside. He pulled out what looked like holo-emitters and a small rectangular box. He assembled the device with confidence and speed.

"What does that thing do?" asked Clarence.

"I don't really have a name for it, but it's a 3D Emulator," answered Tyler. "I developed a program that converts the coded signals within the entire system's network into a virtual world using an enhanced 3D fractal algorithm."

"A 3D what?" asked Clarence.

"It's easier for me to show you rather than try to explain it," said Tyler.

With that, he switched on the machine. A huge holo-screen lit up one side of the room. It was similar to the ones Clarence used from his workstation, except this one was much larger. Tyler rummaged through his bag again and pulled out a pair of black gloves, except that these were not ordinary gloves. These gloves had shiny black filaments embedded within the fabric, with pad-like nodes at the knuckle joints and fingertips. The gloves were activated when Tyler touched the inside of each palm with its corresponding middle finger.

With the gloves activated, Tyler moved his hands up to the large holo-screen and began manipulating the virtual environment manually. By keeping his palms open and moving them deliberately in certain directions, he navigated through the network like an expert. To Clarence, it looked like Tyler was searching for something. In the virtual environment, he approached an area that looked like a huge hole in the fabric of the network.

"This is where the breach occurred." Tyler zoomed in on the node and revealed a serial number and the exact port where the errant code was smuggled in. "Must have been a microdrive, because the third port was the point of entry."

A barely perceptible red crystalline trail starting from the compromised port lead to one of the waste management subsystems. Using his right hand, Tyler selected an icon from the virtual menu. A swab appeared in the holo-screen which he used to wipe the red crystalline trail. Then he deposited the swab into a virtually hidden panel to the side. A moment later, another holo-window popped up with the analysis results.

"Interesting. A weak code fragment was introduced through the breach. That's strange. How could it have propagated throughout the system?"

Clarence and Victor looked at each other, perplexed. Hell if they knew. They didn't even get as far as the weak code fragment.

"Tell me. What exactly happened after you first noticed the glitch," asked Tyler excitedly.

"As per protocol, we ran a self-repairing diagnostic program. Something new that saved a huge amount of programmer time," answered Clarence eagerly. At least he was able to answer that question.

"Thanks. That helps," said Tyler. He quickly navigated his way to the diagnostics folder and located the program that was used to diagnose and repair the glitches.

The program manifested itself as a purple fifty-eight-sided polygon or a pentacontakaioctagon. He picked it up in his virtual hands and tossed it into the analyzer. Once in the analyzer, he activated a simulation of what it would do to the inactive code fragment.

What spewed out of the simulator surprised Tyler, making him jump back a foot. His heart pounded from the shock, and he paused to catch his breath. A red blob with multiple sticky tentacles squirted out of the simulator. When it hit the network fabric, it used its tentacles to move from system to system.

"See those tentacles?" asked Tyler, addressing both Clarence and Victor. His face showed both anxiety and pride.

"Yes," answered the two spectators in unison. They were mesmerized by the show and were hard pressed to quell their enthusiasm.

"That's the SNFR component, or the sniffer part of my original program. This is ingenious," said Tyler with more admiration than disgust. "Someone was able to program a dormant virus that can bypass virtually all the safety protocols in existence for these advanced server farms. Not only that, but the diagnostics and self-repairing programs that are meant to clean up these viruses, served as a catalytic converter to transform these code fragments into something else."

"What does that mean?" asked Victor. Like everyone else, he was starting to get suspicious about what was actually going on. "The system has been cleaned, hasn't it?"

"Not from what I can see from the simulation," answered Tyler.

"If the self-repairing diagnostic program didn't clean out the virus, then where did they go? Why are the systems running normally now?" asked Clarence. Although curious, he was afraid to hear the answers.

"Those are good questions," said Tyler. "Now that we know what the virus looks like, I can build a virtual filter so that we can see what is exactly happening in the systems."

Tyler hit another menu and configured a screening filter by picking up the red blob simulation and tossing it at the virtual filter. It went splat against the filter like an insect hitting an ultraviolet bug lamp, then merged with it. Tyler affixed the filter onto a virtual beam emitter which he picked up and held in his virtual hands like a flashlight. While navigating the government's divisional computer systems, it was apparent that the red viral blobs had dispersed themselves throughout the entire system.

As he approached each blob, he pressed a red button on the beam emitter, which sent out a death ray that dried up the red blobs and turned them into virtual red dust. He did this for each system, travelling from one end to the next. As the day wore on, Tyler started looking more and more perplexed. "Hmmm."

"What is it?" asked Victor, a worried expression on his face.

"This is odd. As I go further and further along, I'm finding dying or dead viruses. Doesn't make sense. Why go through the trouble of designing something with a failure to thrive?" Tyler paused to think. "Unless…"

"That's a good question," said Clarence. "You'd think they had a target in mind."

"Wait. What did you say?" asked Tyler.

"I said that's a good question."

"No, what did you say after that?"

"I said you'd think they had a target in mind."

"Oh crap, that's it," exclaimed Tyler. "Why didn't I think of this before?"

"Think of what?" asked Clarence.

"The sniffer component," said Tyler. "It's designed to sniff out specific targets. With some minor tweaks, you can narrow down the targets even more."

"It'll take you days to narrow down and locate the specific target," said Clarence.

"Have you not met my 3D Emulator?" asked Tyler with prideful sarcasm.

Clarence remained silent, not knowing where Tyler was going with this.

Tyler pulled up the menu and zoomed out, putting the entire virtual computer system within view in the holo-screen.

All three men gasped at the same time. One section of the government computer system was completely red, covered entirely with the virus. The whole financial sector, credit records, banking processes, the foundation that drove the day to day activities of the government were in jeopardy.

Clarence backed away slowly to locate the nearest phone. "We need to call the President, now!"

-To be continued in Book 2-

If you enjoyed this title, I would appreciate your leaving a review of the book. Good reviews encourage an author to write as well as help books to sell. Good reviews can be just a few short sentences describing what you liked about the book without having a spoiler. If you could spend 30 seconds writing a review, I would appreciate it: you can review this title right now at your favorite retailer.

Here is a preview of the **next story** you may enjoy:

VICTOR NUGENT and Tyler Wilkens just stood there, astonished, while Clarence Rainer made the urgent call to the President's office.

The tech team had discovered a massive viral infestation within the World Government's financial sector computer systems. The President's office startled them even more by granting them Carte Blanche to deal with the situation. With a massive government payment due within the week, they weren't taking any chances.

"Hold on," said Wilkens. He approached one of the viral blobs. It reacted to his touch. Using his virtual hands, Wilkens picked up the quivering mass. It felt oozy in his hands, like a mass of gelatin. Swiping his hand from left to right, a virtual window popped up. He selected the magnifying glass function, and the image of the blob zoomed up on the screen. He examined it from all angles. But when he looked underneath the blob, there appeared a circular greenish glow. It was pulsating.

"Now this is interesting," said Wilkens excitedly. "I didn't expect this."

"What do you see?" asked Victor, confused.

"I configured my rendering software to pick out certain code fragments that I've identified in my programming sequences," said Wilkens. "See that pulsating green glow underneath this virus?"

Both men uttered at the same time, "Uh huh."

"Well, that's the kill code that I put in my programming," said Wilkens. "It's no secret that hackers and certain programmers will put secret backdoors or kill switches into their programs. I put in a kill-switch fragment in my coding. Only I know about it. Anyone mimicking or trying to build other viruses, even weaponized ones, will end up incorporating a kill code that renders the virus inert."

"What does that mean for us?" asked Clarence.

"Watch this," said Wilkens. He opened the virtual utility folder and pulled out an eyedropper which he placed onto the glowing pulsating greenish glow. He squeezed the bulbous part of the dropper and suctioned up some of the glowing essence. He activated another folder, pulled out a device, and inserted the dropper.

The device had a numerical keypad with selection display. Wilkens scrolled down the selection bar and highlighted Dispersion Grenade. He set the numerical counter at 1,000. Then he pressed the <RUN> button. In a matter of moments, dispersion grenades started popping out of the device.

"This is it. Everybody, pick up as many grenades as you can handle and put them into your rucksacks. I'll show you how to use them," said Wilkens.

After the device finished producing the full number of grenades and they were packed away, Wilkens and the group moved on to each virus-infected virtual corridor. He plucked a grenade out of his rucksack and pulled the pin.

"Although we're in a virtual environment, you should plug your ears and take shelter. You'll have only a few seconds to find cover once you launch," said Wilkens.

"Do as I do when we're in the vicinity of these viruses," said Wilkens. He tossed the activated grenade into the center of the infected corridor.

The team ducked around the hallway from the main corridor where the grenade was dropped. A split second later, a boom sounded, and they felt the virtual chamber shudder. Wilkens peeked around the wall to assess the damage. He signaled for the others to join him.

"The coast is clear. It's safe to come out," said Wilkens.

The group emerged back onto the corridor, but now all they saw was the red goo of the destroyed viruses throughout the corridor. They were annihilated. The gooey mass was fast turning into red dust, falling and disintegrating into nothing. The corridor was completely clear of the virus.

"Now all we have to do is proceed throughout the financial section of this computer system to clear the entire mess of viruses there. With the three of us, we should be able to rid the system of the virus in a matter of hours."

If you enjoyed this sample then look for **Kill Code: The Cyber Heist Files - Book 2**.

Here is a preview of **another story** you may also enjoy:

Stinger Jacked

THE ASSAULT ship sat in the makeshift bay pending a software upgrade after an emergency landing for repairs. The cold, dry wind howled relentlessly, serving as a cloak for a pending clandestine operation.

Specialist Joseph Brunner remained crouched in the shadows. The rest of the members of the six-person tactical team were hidden, awaiting the order from their leader, Garon Rogal, to board the scantily guarded vessel.

Their mission, to steal an intact Stinger Class assault ship from the ka'Thar, was crazy, to say the least. Even crazier was breaking into an OmniClon Universal (OCU) outpost to do it. The resistance knew that the OCU had state-of-the-art equipment, making the task nearly impossible. Also, they had access to advanced technology supplied by their alliance partner, the ka'Thar. Essentially, the team had volunteered for a suicide mission.

In desperation, the Free Humanity Movement (FHM), the resistance force fighting for the liberation of humanity represented as the Versapiens, had hastily sent a small team to hijack the ship. No one had ever accomplished such a feat, and nothing this risky had even been attempted. The resistance had lost entire tactical teams to less daunting missions. But the grand prize made the cost in lives worth the risk.

Brunner was not supposed to be there. He had not planned his life that way. Although he volunteered to fight for the resistance, he never wanted to be a soldier.

He thought he could contribute somehow in other ways. With a genius IQ, Brunner was more comfortable behind a desk, punching away on a keyboard, building computer models, programming, and analyzing data.

But today, the FHM did not need him behind a desk. Instead, they needed his on-the-fly expertise with uploading a virus into the target ship's system to allow the small tactical team the ability to access the core systems and steal the ship. Brunner's skills were needed for a critical role in the mission. The pressure he felt was beyond anything he had ever experienced.

Twenty-Four Hours Earlier

"Can we trust this intel?" asked Lieutenant Garon Rogal.

"It's good. I vouch for the source with my life," answered Herm Mellitz, the Intelligence Officer.

"We need you to put a team together, and do it fast," said Commander Statton. "You have a twenty-four-hour window before the ship joins the ranks of the OCU's regular fleet. There is no telling when we'll get such an opportunity again."

Rogal furrowed his brows. The intel was like a gift from heaven, and it would be a waste not to act on it. It wasn't every day a ka'Thar ship required emergency service from an OCU outpost. Especially from an easily accessible outpost with an established routine. He perceived many areas of concern. This could be their first and last opportunity to acquire an assault ship of their own. If they failed, their hand would be revealed, and the OCU would surely tighten up security measures to counter any future attempts.

"Under normal circumstances, it would take at least a month to plan and train for such a mission, and the outcome at best would be eighty percent successful," said Rogal. "But these aren't normal circumstances. We've been hit hard by the OCU, losing over fifty percent of our forces these past six months." His demeanor hardened, having warned Command against squandering resources needlessly in low-yield, high-casualty missions.

If you enjoyed this sample then look for **Stinger Jacked**.

Other Books by Freddie Kim

- The Time Guardian Thriller Series

- Stinger Jacked

Get the latest update on new releases from the author at:

https://www.freddiekim.com/newsletter/

About the Author - Freddie Kim

As a child, Freddie Kim would make blanket forts and refrigerator-box space ships, both essential things needed to repel against invasion from an alien race. Freddie has never really grown up from his childhood fantasies. The inspiration that he draws from the memories of his youth is captured and revealed to all in his writing.

Connect with Freddie Kim

I really appreciate you reading my book! Here are my social media coordinates:

Friend me on Facebook:
https://www.facebook.com/FreddieKimAuthor/

Follow me on Twitter:
https://twitter.com/freddiekimauth1

Check me out on Goodreads:
https://www.goodreads.com/author/show/16961603.Freddie_Kim

Subscribe to my newsletter:
https://www.freddiekim.com/newsletter/

Visit my website: https://www.freddiekim.com/